The Totally Terrifying Three

For John, who always gets me with his diagonals - H.O.

For my Totally Terrifying Three: Tanja, Monika and Luka - D.M.

First published in hardback in 2011 by Hodder Children's Books
First published in paperback in 2012

Hodder Children's Books, 338 Euston Road, London, NW1 3BH
Hodder Children's Books Australia, Level 17/207 Kent Street, Sydney, NSW 2000

A catalogue record of this book is available from the British Library.

ISBN 978 1 444 90303 4

Printed in China

Hodder Children's Books is a division of Hachette Children's Books,
an Hachette UK Company

www.hachette.co.uk

The Totally Terrifying Three

Hiawyn Oram
and
David Melling

A division of Hachette Children's Books

The Totally Terrifying Three

Once there was a Dragon who was convinced he was TOTALLY TERRIFYING.

One look at himself in the mirror and he nearly jumped out of his skin.

"TOTALLY TERRIFYING DRAGON ALERT!"

he'd shout before he went anywhere which only made everyone dash, dive or RUN for their lives.

One day he said to
his little pet Wiggles,
"We're out of here. I can't keep
on like this, frightening my
neighbours out of their wits."

Wiggles raised his eyes to the skies
but he helped the Dragon pack
and off they set.

It wasn't long before they came upon a Witch
scaring herself silly in her magic mirror.

"TOTALLY TERRIFYING WITCH ALERT!"

she screeched as soon as she saw them.

"Don't look at me if you want to keep your socks on!"

"Hold on a moment," said the Dragon.
"I'm the frightening one around here.
At the sight of me, giants' knees knock
and mountains turn to jelly."

"Well, you don't scare me," said the Witch.
"I don't!" said the Dragon.
"In that case we should go along together."

So they went along together and they hadn't gone far before they came upon a Giant terrifying himself in his mini car mirror.

“TOTALLY TERRIFYING GIANT ALERT!”

he roared as soon as he saw them.

“Don’t look at me
if you want to keep
your hair on!”

"Hang on a tiddly tad," said the Dragon,
"we're the scary ones in the neighbourhood.
We scare the pants off people and the spots off the spotted ones."

“Well, you don’t scare me,”
said the Giant.

“We don’t?” said the Dragon.
“In that case we should go along
together.”

So they went along together and they hadn't gone far before they stopped for a picnic and came upon a Toddler.

Her name was Not-So-Tiddly and she didn't say a lot but whatever she said made sense.

“Nice Giant, nice Giant,” she cooed. “Give me a ride on your shoulders so I can see what I can’t see from toddling.”

Well, no one ever called that Giant nice if they knew what was good for them, but a Toddler is a Toddler so he gave her a ride on his shoulders.

And when he put her down, she toddled over to the Witch and gurgled, "Sweet Witch, sweet Witch, give me a fly on your broomstick so I can know what I can't know from toddling."

Well, no one called that Witch sweet if they wanted to see another birthday, but a Toddler is a Toddler so she gave her a fly on her broomstick.

And when the Witch brought her down, Not-So-Tiddly toddled over to the Dragon and babbled, "Dear Dragon, dear Dragon, sing me a sweet song, a lullaby, so I can dream what I can't dream while toddling."

At once, the Dragon settled her in his arms and sang her the only lullaby he knew.

And when she was fast asleep he tiptoed over and gently laid her down in the buttercups.

Then he strode back to the others and said, "Well, here's the thing. We don't scare each other, and we don't scare Not-So-Tiddly, so who do we scare?"

"Take a new look," barked Wiggles.

And now when they looked, they saw themselves as they'd been with Not-So-Tiddly...

...and nearly jumped out of their skins in surprise.

"I'm certainly silly," said the Witch, "but not one bit scary."

"I'm generally jowly," said the Giant, "but gi-normously jolly."

"And I'm an itsy on the ugly side, but totally UNterrifying," said the Dragon.

"Why, like this, we could go along forever scaring absolutely NOBODY!"

And when we last heard, that's just what they were doing –
– going around together with a sign that said:

Although once in a while and strictly for the fun of it they still enjoyed...

...scaring the socks off
THEMSELVES!